The Little Pet Dragon

"A greyhound!" James said in absolute wonder. "A greyhound puppy!"

James bent down and stroked the dragon's hard snouty head, but he did not feel scales – he felt soft, silky fur. The dragon looked up at him adoringly and tried to wag its tail in a greyhound-like way. James smoothed under its chin where its softer skin was a pale lime colour and felt a string tied around its neck. On the string was a label, and on the label was some black, spiky, magical-looking writing.

Another Young Hippo Magic story to enjoy:

The Marmalade Pony
Linda Newbery

Or dare you try a Young Hippo Spooky?

Scarem's House
Malcolm Yorke

The Screaming Demon Ghostie
Jean Chapman

Ready for a Young Hippo Adventure?

Henry to the Rescue and Other Stories
Ruth Silvestre

Young Hippo Adventures for confident readers:

The Outfit Series –
The Secret of Weeping Wood
We Didn't Mean To, Honest!
Robert Swindells

PHILIPPA GREGORY

The Little Pet Dragon

Illustrated by David Wyatt

For Victoria and Adam

Scholastic Children's Books,
Scholastic Publications Ltd,
7-9 Pratt Street, London NW1 0AE, UK

Scholastic Inc.,
555 Broadway, New York, NY 10012-3999, USA

Scholastic Canada Ltd,
123 Newkirk Road, Richmond Hill,
Ontario, Canada L4C 3G5

Ashton Scholastic Pty Ltd,
P O Box 579, Gosford, New South Wales,
Australia

Ashton Scholastic Ltd,
Private Bag 92801, Penrose, Auckland,
New Zealand

First published in the UK by Scholastic Publications Ltd, 1994

ISBN 0 590 55784 X

Typeset by Contour Typesetters, Southall, London
Printed by Cox & Wyman Ltd, Reading, Berks.

10 9 8 7 6 5

Chapter 1

James Alastair lived in a small red-brick house, part of a terrace of houses in a little town beside the North Sea. All his life he had wanted a greyhound. Greyhounds are long lean dogs: tremendously fast runners that are sometimes trained to be racers and win prizes for their owners. James Alastair dreamed of owning a racing greyhound. He dreamed of owning the fastest greyhound in the world.

One day – the day before his ninth birthday – James was walking along the street on his way home from school, wondering what his mother and father would give him for his present. He knew it would not be a greyhound, and he was afraid that it would not be a bicycle either. Everyone in his class had a bicycle except James. Suddenly, he stopped.

There, on the pavement in front of him, was a wooden basket – the sort that gardeners use for carrying small plants and trowels. Inside it, coiled up very small, was a little animal. It had a little snouty face like a tiny crocodile, but much smileyer. It had

round nostrils and loving, deep amber eyes. It had two sharp ears that stood up, rather like a horse's. It had a fat little body covered in scales and a long, long tail like nothing in the world. Running down its spine was a row of hard, triangle-shaped spikes. Its plump feet had sharp golden claws. It was a bright emerald green. It was shimmering all over with the light of a very strong magic spell. James could hardly see it for the power of the magic spell. Instead he saw the very thing he wanted most in the world.

"A greyhound!" James said in absolute wonder. "A greyhound puppy!"

James bent down and stroked the dragon's hard snouty head, but he did not feel scales – he felt soft, silky fur. The dragon looked up at him adoringly and tried to wag its tail in a greyhound-like way. James smoothed under its chin where its softer skin was a pale lime colour and felt a string tied around its neck. On the string was a label, and on the label was some black, spiky, magical-looking writing. It said:

Please look after this little Pet Dragon.
I made him by accident and now
he needs a home.
You can name him whatever you like.

signed

Meehort the Wizard

James rubbed his eyes and read the label again. But even as he was reading it the letters were swimming around like fish in a pond. The second time he read it, the message was completely different:

Please look after this little greyhound puppy. He has no mother or father, and he needs a home. You can name him whatever you like.

signed

Meehort the Wizard

Of course, James was delighted. He picked up the gardener's basket with the small green dragon inside. It was very light, no heavier than a greyhound puppy. He carried it home in his arms and put it carefully on the kitchen table.

His mother and father were out. James thought carefully about what they might say when they saw his surprising new pet. He rather hoped they would be absolutely delighted. He rather knew that they would not.

James put his head on one side and looked at the little dragon. He saw the most beautiful fawn-coloured greyhound puppy. The dragon put *its* head on one side too and looked back at James. It saw a nine-year-old boy (well, very nearly nine), rather small for his age, with a dirty face and a wide smile with a gap where a tooth was missing.

"You're my greyhound puppy," James said to him. "I'm going to keep you whatever anyone says."

Just then, the back door opened and his mother came in from the garden. James hastily pulled a tea towel over his new pet's snouty little head. All that showed was one marigold eye.

"What on earth are you doing with that trug?" asked James's mother. "I've just wiped the table."

The little green dragon hidden under the tea towel looked surprised. He didn't mind being called a greyhound but you could tell from the hurt look in his rose-amber eyes that he didn't like being called a trug.

"Look, Mam!" James said, paying no attention to the wiping of the table or the trug. "A greyhound puppy!" He flung back the tea towel and the little dragon sat up.

James's mother looked in the basket and her face went warm and tender. The magician's magic was wonderfully powerful. All she saw was a fawn-coloured greyhound puppy with long legs and intelligent eyes.

"Isn't he sweet," she said. "I wonder who he belongs to?"

The dragon tried to wag its tail like a greyhound puppy.

"Can I keep it?" James asked. "Can I please, Mam? For my birthday? *Please?*"

James's dad had not had a job since the steel mill near their home had closed down. James's mam had to work as a cleaner at an office block at night to earn enough money for the three of them. And there never was enough money, however hard she worked. She had been worrying all day about James's birthday. They did not have enough money to buy him a bicycle so they would have to give him something else, something cheaper, and he would have to pretend to like it. The same thing had happened last year as well.

It made her want to cry when she had to say "no" to James. It made her face look sad and pale when she had to work late at night, pushing a heavy floor polisher over the wooden floor. It made James's dad feel so helpless and so angry that he wanted to dash into the steel mill and open it up and make steel all on his own. But of course he could not. It made all three of them miserable.

"We can't afford to feed him," she said. It was true. They had hardly enough money to feed themselves, and they never had any treats. They never had steak or ice-cream or cakes from the shop. They never had holidays away from home.

The dragon bunched itself up to look tiny, and peered up at James's mother. His little green face seemed to promise that he would eat hardly a thing.

As he moved, James saw something glinting in the basket under the dragon. He pulled it out. It was a large golden guinea coin from the olden days. Stuck to it, with a blob of red sealing-wax marked with a special magic-looking seal, was another note in the spiky black handwriting, that said:

This is for his keep. He can eat dog food if you insist. But he likes flowers in Summertime.

This was all rather odd. And the oddest thing of all was that James's mother didn't seem a bit surprised.

"There's your dad's garden in flower all the summer long," she said.

James's father was a brilliant gardener. Their street backed on to the allotments where there was a huge old derelict greenhouse. It had once been the greenhouse in the gardens of a grand manor house. But now the gardens had become allotments and the greenhouse was empty and just used as a store. Everyone in the street had an allotment and grew vegetables.

James's dad was different. He grew the vegetables that they needed for eating, but all around the borders of the vegetable patch he grew flowers. He loved flowers. He grew roses and daisies, chrysanthemums, great big ragged-headed dahlias, and small, sweet-smelling lilies of the valley. His favourite flowers were the wild and wonderful orchids that will only grow in the islands of the South Seas. James's dad would look at pictures of orchids in books and dream about growing them.

It was an impossible dream, for orchids have to be kept very warm and the only place James's dad had for delicate plants was the kitchen window-sill. Indeed, all the window-

sills in James's house were already crowded with pots with little shoots growing in them.

"The gold coin will pay for his dog food!" James said excitedly. "So can we keep him, Mam? Can we? For my birthday?"

James's mam looked from James's excited face to the dragon's appealing little eyes.

"Yes!" she said suddenly. "Why not!"

All at once James felt reckless and brave.

Why not? Why *shouldn't* they do something exciting and daring that would make them all feel happy?

"*Yes!*" he shouted, and he dashed out to the allotment, to find his dad and tell him that they had a pet – a wonderful greyhound puppy who might grow up to be a champion racer.

"He certainly has the looks for it," his dad said when he came in, all breathless, with James tugging at his muddy hand. "See how intelligent his eyes are?" The little dragon's eyes went dark with happiness from a yellowy-amber until they were red as coals with his eagerness.

"See how long and thin his body is?" said James's dad. "That's a good sign."

The little dragon stretched out to his full length. His spiky tail hung over the edge of the basket. It had a hard little triangle at the end. But it was very powerful magic indeed, for no one saw a dragon at all. They all saw a greyhound puppy.

"He's a champion!" James's dad said.

He lifted the little dragon out of the trug and put him gently down on the kitchen floor. The little dragon waddled over to where the central heating boiler stood in the corner of the kitchen. It was warm and it hummed softly. Perhaps it reminded him of the inside of his eggshell when he was a little baby dragon, not yet hatched. He flumped down on the floor beside it and smiled at them with his rosy eyes all misty and contented.

"We'll get him a dog basket and keep it there," James's mam said, pleased. "I'll give him a box just for now."

They found a cardboard box for him, and lined it with one of James's dad's old holey jumpers. The dragon sat quietly in the box as if he had lived with them all his life.

"Tomorrow," James's mam said, "we'll take him to the vet for his injections."

Chapter 2

The visit to the vet was not a great success.

"This is a very strange sort of dog. What breed is it?" asked the vet, looking very sternly at James and his mam over the top of her spectacles. "I have never seen such a dog in my life before."

The dragon curled up tighter in his basket and looked at her with anxious yellow eyes.

"We thought it was a greyhound puppy," James's mam said.

The vet shook her head. "Definitely not," she said.

Magic does not seem to work very well on vets. She could see that he was not a pedigree greyhound, but she could not see exactly what he was.

"He must be some kind of mongrel," she said.

The vet ran her skilled hands over the dragon and she felt fur. She pulled at the hard scaly skin at the dragon's neck and tried to inject him. The needle broke at once and the injection liquid squirted into James's hair.

"Gracious!" said the vet, amazed. "That must be a faulty needle. I *am* sorry. Are you all right?"

"Yes!" said James. "Yes, yes."

The dragon's little face looked old and wise. He had not understood what they wanted to do to him. Now he knew. When the vet had the next injection ready he quickly stretched so that there was a tiny opening between the scales on his neck. The needle slipped in easily. He let out a little squeak (baby dragons are not very brave) and James rubbed his head.

"There," the vet said. "Don't let him walk on the pavements until he has had a booster shot."

The little pet dragon's eyes went quite primrose with dismay at this, but he sat very still in his basket while James carried it out of the surgery to the bus stop.

"It *is* my birthday today, Mam," he said quietly at the bus stop. "Even if he is a mongrel you won't take him away from me, will you?"

His mam sniffed. "I don't think she knew what she was talking about," she said defiantly. "He looks like a greyhound to your dad and me. He'll be a greyhound to us. What shall we call him?"

James thought for a moment. Ever since the vet had doubted that his pet was a real true-bred pedigree greyhound he had been wanting to give him a real doggy name, to make it clear to everyone what he was.

"Lassie," he said. "We'll call him Lassie the Wonder Dog."

That should settle any doubts, he thought, pleased. No one could doubt that his pet was a true-bred dog if he answered to the name of Lassie the Wonder Dog.

Lassie the little pet dragon soon learned to come when he was called. He learned to walk to heel. He learned to fetch sticks. He tried his best to bark. When he went out for a walk with James or his dad or his mam he walked on a lead and sat at the kerb while they waited to cross the road. Never in the entire history of dragons did a little green dragon try harder to be a dog.

And it worked. It might have been magic, or it might have been that people just don't expect to see dragons walking nicely to heel or tied to the lamppost outside the corner shop. Pretty soon everyone in the streets all around James's home knew that Lassie was James's dog and that he might one day be a prizewinning racing greyhound.

Spring came, and James's dad decided that they could start Lassie's training. Every afternoon, after school, James, his dad and Lassie would go to the wide, flat stretch of grass which ran between the sea wall and the sea road. In summertime all the men would bring their dogs out there to race them, one against the other. They had a little machine – a box with an engine and a long rope which pulled a bundle of cloth very quickly in front of the racing dogs. The dogs all thought it was a hare or a rabbit and chased after it. The winner was the first one past the finishing line.

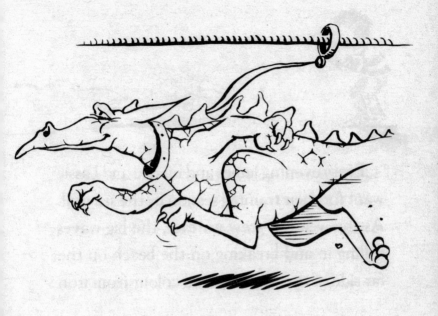

James and his dad started training Lassie by running alongside him, but he was much too fast for them. In the end they stretched out a long rope and James stood at one end and his dad at the other. They clipped Lassie's lead to the rope to make sure that he could not get away, and then they called Lassie from one end to the other.

Every evening James and his dad and Lassie
went for their training session by the sea wall.
As the weather grew warmer, the big waves
rolling in and breaking on the beach on the
far side of the wall changed colour from iron

grey to blue, and the cold wind that blew off the sea grew warmer and gentler. Very soon Lassie was running from James to his dad and back again without a rope or a lead. Soon they could take him down to the wide dry sand of the beach and let him run and run and run.

No one had seen a young dog run as fast or as far as Lassie. Every day he got faster and faster. He grew sleek and well muscled, his chest grew wider, his tummy grew slimmer and his eyes shone. He gave up eating tinned dog food and started eating flowers. James's dad brought him the fading heads of daffodils, and then the bluebells from the little garden.

When summer came and the allotment borders were filled with flowers, Lassie was allowed out to graze on whatever he liked. He never ate the buds, and if James's dad asked him to leave one particular plant alone, he never forgot. They had a tiny patch of grass in the back garden and James did not have to mow it once that summer. The dragon went along it, nibbling away at the tops of the grass and the daisy petals.

By the middle of June, Lassie looked like a beautiful dog in the prime of condition. A lot of the men who owned racing greyhounds had seen him in training and they kept asking James and his dad to come along one evening and race Lassie against their dogs. James used to love to see his dad smile and put them off. "When the time is right," he said wisely. "He's a young dog as yet. We don't want to rush him."

"I think you have a proper champion on your hands there," one of the men told him. "You bring him for a race against our dogs and if he wins we'll all help you train him. He'd be a credit to us."

James's dad finally agreed. "Next month, then," he said.

Chapter 3

Every kid in James's school came to the sea front to watch Lassie race. It was nearly the end of the school term and it felt as if the summer holidays had come early. Every mam who had nothing better to do that day strolled out to see Lassie race, and they brought the little kids in their pushchairs and the babies in their prams. An ice-cream van

saw the crowd and stopped on the sea road and played the tune so loudly that all the kids with pocket money queued up for ice-creams, and those that didn't have any money swapped everything they could think of for a lick.

Every man who owned a greyhound, or had once had a greyhound, or thought he might get one some day, was there. Some of the very old men could remember when the little town had bred a champion greyhound before, and they kept taking people by the arm and telling them all about it. It was quite a crowd and in the centre of it all, envied by everyone, smiling so wide that you could see the gap in his teeth, was James holding Lassie on a beautiful new red collar and lead which his mam had given him last night. She had been saving up for it for three weeks.

Lassie's eyes were bright and alert. His ears pricked up with excitement. He understood exactly what they wanted him to do and he loved running races. He was so excited that he could feel a hot smoky feeling building up inside him. He gave a little gasp and a tiny cloud of smoke puffed out of his nostrils. Lassie sniffed it back inside quickly, before anyone noticed. He knew very well that promising young greyhounds do not breathe fire.

James knelt down beside him and lovingly pulled his ears. "Now don't get frightened," he said. "Just try your hardest. If you don't win, it doesn't matter. We just want to see how well you do."

The little dragon's heart burned with love. He had to hold his breath to stop the smoke leaking out. He looked at James with his warm amber eyes. Nothing in the world

could stop him winning the race, he thought. He was absolutely determined to win the race for James.

There was a race for other dogs before it was Lassie's turn. James turned to watch them. The men put their dogs into a row of little boxes, fastened the doors, and stepped back. The dogs looked out through the front of the boxes, some of them whining with excitement and eagerness. Someone started the machine which whipped away the little bundle of cloth down the grass. The front doors of the boxes all flew open together and the dogs raced down the track, chasing the cloth, towards the machine where their owners caught them.

"If he wins here we could enter him at a proper greyhound racing track," James's dad said. "We could go all around the country, racing with him. And he could win money too. A prizewinning greyhound is a wonderful animal. He'll get his picture in the papers. We'll be famous."

Lassie could feel the heat burning and burning inside him. There was a cool breeze blowing gently off the sea. He turned his nose towards it and let out a little puff of smoke. He was so excited he could hardly bear to wait.

"Our turn now," James's dad said at last. "You can put him in the hutch, James."

44

Very gently James directed Lassie into the hutch. Lassie peered out through the grille at the front. He could see James and James's dad walking up to the finishing line. He could see James's mam standing with her friends. He could see all the kids from James's school getting ready to cheer. He could feel a huge smoky excited warmth growing in his tummy, and then he could feel a strange itchy bursty feeling on either shoulder.

He tried to concentrate on what was happening. Someone was resetting the machine, then they pulled the little bundle of cloth towards the hutches and the other dogs barked and whined. Lassie couldn't quite see the point of chasing a duster, but it was obvious that James wanted him to chase it, so he would. Someone shouted "Ready?" And someone else called back "Ready!" Then the grille on the front of the hutch flew

open and Lassie leaped out.

He was ahead of the other dogs in a few quick strides. The bundle of cloth was whizzing away from him. Lassie put down his sleek head and raced after it, his paws pounding on the smooth turf. The legs of the school kids, the wheels of the pushchairs, the feet of the grown-ups all flashed past him as he ran faster than he had ever run before. He could feel his breath coming in hot smoky

gasps, and his heart pounding faster than his paws. Then there was a rush and a bang and he was at the finish line and he heard James's excited yell: "Lassie! Oh, Lassie! You won!"

But he was too excited to stop, and the smoking feeling in his tummy was too hot, and the itchy feelings on his shoulders were too much for him. He ran past James, diving under his outstretched hands. He dashed on and on, down the sea front, unstoppable, uncatchable, the fastest greyhound that there had ever been in the history of the world. And as he ran he heard a wonderful powerful ripple of sound as two curtains of green wings finally burst from his shoulders and opened on either side of his body. Then he was not running any more but his feet were racing through air, and the ground was falling away below him and the salty cool wind was buoying him upwards and upwards.

His wings were beating strongly and smoothly and Lassie the little pet dragon was a fully-fledged dragon – flying free, soaring, as high as a party balloon, as high as a kite, as high as a glider, as high as an aeroplane – higher, higher, higher, past small surprised sparrows, past soaring seagulls, past all the birds until he was a little black dot circling high in the pale evening sky.

"Lassie!" James yelled, suddenly afraid, suddenly terrified. "Lassie! Come back! Don't leave me Lassie! Don't go!"

In utter horror James watched his pet – the pet that only a moment ago was certain to be a champion greyhound – circle and turn in the empty sky. James watched him soar and wheel, as if to get his bearings, and then he beat his wings strongly and headed away, away from the sea front, away from the cold chimneys of the derelict steel mill, away from James's little house with the allotments and the old greenhouse behind it, away towards the west and the setting sun.

James forgot about his friends and all the grown-ups who were staring open-mouthed at the sky. He threw himself face down on the grass and wept as if his heart was breaking.

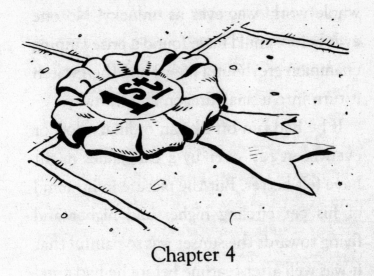

Chapter 4

James did not go home at once, he felt too miserable. While his mam and dad walked slowly home, arm in arm, very quiet and sad, and everyone else stood around at the sea front chattering and pointing in the air and marvelling at what they had just seen, James went the long way round, by the back alleys where no one would see him and notice his red eyes and muddy face. Surely no one in the whole world was ever as unlucky! No one ever before could have found a prizewinning champion greyhound puppy and then watch it turn into a small dragon and fly away.

If he had run off like an ordinary dog, or even been run over by a car, James might have felt better. But the picture in his mind of his pet circling higher and higher and flying towards the sunset was so painful that it was well after teatime before he had cried enough on his own and felt able to go home and face the sympathy of his mam and dad.

But when he came around the corner into his street he knew at once that something else had happened. His dad was out in the street staring up at the sky, and all the neighbours were out too. The whole street seemed to be there, looking upwards and pointing. The little kids were jumping up and down and yelling encouragement. But the grown-ups were looking worried. James rubbed the last of the tears from his face and ran up to his dad and pulled at his sleeve.

"It's Lassie," Dad said, his hand shielding his eyes from the setting sun as he squinted upwards. He didn't even glance down at James. "He's having trouble landing. He tried to land in the street but he clipped the lamppost. He seems to have grown very big."

James felt like leaping in the air himself. His pet was coming home like a huge green homing pigeon! Lassie had not run away – he

was coming home to where he belonged. It was wonderful. It was as big a miracle as finding him in the first place. Lassie wanted to come back. It was magic!

"Look out!" James's dad yelled suddenly. "Here he comes!"

People screamed and ran for their front doors. Lassie loomed down on them like a great green airship. James could see the pale green of his big belly, his claws outstretched as if he were trying to grab on to the air to slow himself up. James could see his wide frightened eyes as he scorched overhead. A few panicky puffs of orange smoke came from his mouth.

He seemed to see James and draw courage from him. He headed straight for the roof of James's house. One desperate forepaw grabbed for the television aerial, the other snatched at the chimney-pot. With a terrible tearing sound, the TV aerial was ripped loose and the chimney-pot wobbled. Lassie balanced for a brief second on the very top of the roof and then they heard the eerie unknown call of a dragon wailing in distress as he slid down the roof on the far side. Then they heard an awful crash as he smashed into the next-door neighbour's garden shed.

James and his dad tore round into the back garden. It looked as if a hurricane had come through it.

The fence between them and next door was squashed flat. The little shed where Mr

Perkins next door kept his lawnmower was smashed to pieces. Slates were trickling off the roof and dropping into the garden like falling rain. Amid all the chaos and confusion was Lassie, looking half-ashamed and half-proud. After all, it *was* his first ever landing. And he was only a very young dragon.

"Lassie!" James shrieked and rushed at him.

Lassie's huge snouty head – he really had grown a lot – turned towards James and the dragon rubbed his head hard against the boy's skinny chest.

"Oh, Lassie!" James said, half-laughing and half-crying. "I'm so glad to see you! I'm so glad you came back! I thought I'd lost you! I thought you'd gone!"

Lassie's big scaly arms came clumsily around James and held him close. It was like being hugged by a grizzly bear wrapped in tin foil, but James was so pleased to get his pet back that he didn't mind at all. He put his arms as far as he could reach around Lassie's trunk-like neck and hugged him back.

"Very touching, I'm sure," said a sharp, horrid voice. It was beastly Mr Perkins from next door. "But who's going to pay for my garden shed? Who's going to pay for my tomatoes? Who's going to pay for my time and trouble in growing them to have them squashed flat by that thing? And who's going to promise that it will be gone by tomorrow morning or I'm calling the police?"

James clutched Lassie even tighter.

"He can't go!" he said. "He's my pet. He's my . . . he's my . . . he's my greyhound puppy."

It sounded silly even to James. Greyhounds, however fast and intelligent, do not soar over rooftops and crash-land on other people's greenhouses.

Mr Perkins looked sour. "Greyhound rubbish!" he said. "I'll have the law on you! I want full compensation and that animal gone by tomorrow or I'll call the police."

He stamped into his house and slammed the door so hard that another tile slid slowly off his roof and fell with a tinkle on top of the others.

Dad said nothing. James said nothing. Lassie gave a deep, hot sigh.

The back door opened and James's mam came out.

"Come on in, you three," she said kindly. "We'll think of something. Something'll come up. Something usually does."

James's dad shook his head. He looked frightened. James had never seen his dad look afraid before. But the cost of the garden shed alone was more than they had in their savings, and there was the roof to repair as well. All of their joy at the amazing triumphant return of Lassie the little pet

dragon had disappeared. It was like a nightmare in which everything had suddenly gone wrong.

"It's a shame about the shed," said Christine from the garden on the other side.

Her twins leaned over the garden fence and nodded in agreement. "And after your wonderful dragon came back home like that!"

"We'll work it out. We'll find the money,"
James's mam said as they went indoors. But
she didn't say where they would find it.
"We'll borrow it, if we have to." But they
didn't know anyone who had money to lend.
"I'll do an extra shift cleaning, I'll work
Sundays." But they all knew that there were
no extra shifts which she could work, and
even if there had been, office cleaners are
never paid very much. Certainly not enough
for a new garden shed and new tiles for the
roof.

"It's got me beat," Dad said. His voice was tired and sad. He sounded like a man who had run out of hope. James saw him look towards the cold, empty steel mill, the wide mouths of the chimneys gaping at the sky. No one made steel any more in their town.

It was a sad, quiet tea. Lassie tried not to be in the way, coiling himself up tight and holding his breath so as not to let the smoke out. But it was obvious that he was too big for the kitchen.

"He'll have to go, James," his mam said sadly. "I'm sorry, but the house just isn't big enough for us all. And if Mr Perkins wants to be nasty about it he could call the police."

James could feel his chin wobbling and hot, sharp tears stinging behind his eyelids.

"But where can he go, Mam?" he asked in a very small voice.

"We'll try the zoo," Dad said. "Or maybe a wildlife park. Somewhere he could be free. But your mam's right, James – he can't stay with us any more."

James hugged Lassie very tight and went out to the garden. There were a few sweet-smelling wallflowers which had not been squashed when Lassie crash-landed. James picked them for Lassie and brought them in to him.

"If only you could make a living from your gardening," his mam said to his dad. "You grow such lovely flowers on the allotment. And there's that old greenhouse just sitting there."

James's dad shrugged. "You need money to earn money," he said. "I can't afford to buy seeds, and a big greenhouse like that would cost a fortune to heat. There's nothing in the world I'd rather do than grow orchids and send them up the road to sell in Newcastle. But it can't be done. It's not for us."

James's mam nodded. James hugged Lassie again and went slowly up the stairs. He felt so miserable that he even cleaned his teeth properly and put out his light at once, without reading by the light of his torch under the bedcovers. It was worse than losing Lassie the first time, if they had to give him away when he had chosen to come home to them. James snuffled a little in sorrow, and fell asleep.

Chapter 5

"Nothing is ever as bad as you expect it to be."

Grown-ups often say that to children to cheer them up when they are dreading something. Sometimes it is true and something is *not* as bad as you thought it would be. On the other hand . . . sometimes it is a good deal worse. It was worse than James could ever have dreamed when he woke in the morning. His mam and his dad were looking serious and the kitchen was looking empty.

"Lassie's gone," his dad said. "Your mam opened the door to let him out into the garden for his morning run and he made a great leap into the air and flew off."

James blinked stupidly. "But he's only just learned to fly," he said. "Just yesterday. He had to run at top speed to take off then. He couldn't just jump up and fly."

"He did though," his mam said. "Straight up, like a big fat butterfly." Her voice shook a little. "I'm sorry," she said. "I didn't think he'd fly off when he'd just come back to us. I'm sorry, James."

"S'all right," James said. Although it wasn't.

James's mam turned her back on James and clattered the mugs as she made tea. James ate his breakfast as if every mouthful was blotting paper.

"D'you think he knew what we were saying?" he asked after a long while. "When you were saying that we couldn't keep him? D'you think he knew we didn't want him? D'you think we hurt his feelings?"

James's mam shook her head. "If he was clever enough to understand what we were saying, then he'd have been clever enough to know we wanted to keep him very much," she said. "He knew we loved him. Perhaps he was always a wild dragon, and he's gone back to wherever he came from."

James nodded and pulled on his jacket, said goodbye to his mam and dad and headed for school. He dawdled all the way along the little road, looking up into the sky and staring at the horizon, but Lassie wasn't there.

He didn't think he'd ever see him again.

James spent the day staring hopelessly out of the school window, watching and waiting to see if Lassie would come home. All evening he sat at his bedroom window watching the sun slowly sink over the allotments till its red light made all the panes of the old greenhouse burn like fire. He sat and watched until the moon rose – a big, golden moon which could have lit Lassie's way home to James. He waited and waited, hoping that at any minute he would see the great ungainly silhouette of his dragon pass across in front of the moon, beating his huge wings.

"You'll catch your death of cold," Mam said. She had been out at her cleaning job and she smelled waxy and sweetly of floor polish. She came into James's bedroom and hugged him tight. "Into bed," she said. "There's nothing to see out there."

The way she spoke told James that she too had been looking up into the night sky as she walked home from work, hoping to see Lassie coming home.

All this time Lassie was flying and flying, like a huge determined green seagull, through the day and through the night. He flew across a great grey tumbling ocean and then flew on, even further. He flew through a rainstorm, when the air seemed to thicken all around him and rain pattered noisily against his scales like rain on a corrugated iron roof. Then it grew light again and the sun came up and the air got warmer. Still Lassie flew on, pointing south, his head stretched before him, his wings beating and beating. The sun grew bright and the sea grew dazzling and blue beneath his dangling feet. Hot air currents swelled under his wings, bearing him up. The winds gathered behind his fat bottom and sped him southward, southward, over a sea which was bluer than any sea Lassie had ever seen.

Over a sea as blue as bluebells, over a sea as blue as delphiniums, and then over a sea as blue as violets Lassie flew until he could see ahead of him a dark smudge on the horizon. The sight gave Lassie energy, and he beat his wings harder, flying strongly towards it. It was a secret island, hidden away from everyone, unknown to any map, with jungle as thick as icing on fudge cake coating the top of the island and tumbling down the sides to beaches of white sand.

Lassie was very tired. He put out his broad feet and let himself flop down on to the soft sand. He stretched his front legs forward and his back legs back, laid his great neck and horny head down on the hot sand and fell fast asleep.

When he awoke it was evening, and above him unknown stars hung in the dark sky like huge yellow lamps. Lassie yawned and sat up

and looked around. He had landed near a stream which trickled through the jungle and then spread out on the sand and oozed away into the sea, like a wet fan. Lassie paddled in the stream, soothing his hot feet and scooping up piles of sand into little sandcastles. When he was tired of playing he

started walking inland, following the course of the stream, wading upstream, pushing his shoulders against the trees and creepers of the jungle, going deeper and deeper, pausing now and then to lap from the water, or to reach up and eat a fragrant hanging flower.

All around him were the secret sounds of the jungle – a squawk from a dreaming parrot, the stirring of a troupe of monkeys, the chatter of night insects, and the quiet gulps of frogs. Lassie's eyes glowed as bright as marmalade. He was very happy. He was not at all afraid of the dark or the strangeness of the place. He knew he was the biggest animal on the whole island – possibly the biggest

animal in the world. And besides, he was a very sweet-tempered dragon. He did not believe that anyone or anything would hurt him, so he was afraid of nothing. His feet in

cool soothing water, his nose questing for the sweetest flowers, Lassie paddled his way inland, to the very heart of the island.

The stream widened ahead of him to make a deep freshwater pool. Lassie sighed with pleasure, a little curl of smoke rising from his nose, and eased himself deep into the water till it lapped over his shoulders and around his outstretched weary wings. On the edge of the pool there was a little hut. Lassie wallowed in the cool stream and soft sandy mud like a great fat green lady in a bubble bath, and watched the door of the hut as it slowly opened.

An old man came out. He wore a gown of deep midnight blue marked with moons and stars and rolling suns and burning comets. In the dark of the jungle the embroidery of his gown glowed with a silver light like a hundred little torches to light his way. On his head was a tall triangular hat. He had a white flowing beard and long white flowing hair. In one thin hand he carried a long silver sceptre.

"Artemis!" he said with pleasure when he saw Lassie. "I sensed that you were coming."

Lassie beamed at him and a little wisp of smoke came through his smiling teeth.

"Grown a good deal, I see," the magician said approvingly. "They must be feeding you well?"

Lassie's eyes were warm at the thought of James, and James's mam and dad.

Meehort the magician nodded. "Dragons *are* expensive to keep," he said. "And little boys even worse. I daresay I should have sent more money for your keep. What shall I do? Send a chest of pirate gold?"

Lassie shook his great head very slowly. Meehort frowned for a moment and then tipped his head on one side as if he were listening.

"Flowers!" he exclaimed. He listened again. "Orchids!" he said. "Well, you've come to the right place for orchids!"

He paused for a few more moments of silence while Lassie stared into his face, nodding his green head and waving his spiny tail in the water.

"Certainly! Certainly!" Meehort said pleasantly. "I'll get you a sack."

He went back into the hut and came out again with a very small paper bag in his hand. Lassie looked at it with his knobbly little eyebrows raised.

Meehort chuckled. "It's bigger than it looks," he said.

Lassie took the little bag in one great green paw.

"Pick Your Own," Meehort said pleasantly. "Help yourself. Eat some flowers before you go, Artemis; it's a long flight home." He patted Lassie's scaly neck and then turned and went towards his little hut.

"Come again," he said. "Any time. My gosh, you *have* shot up, haven't you? And out. And along."

He waved kindly to Lassie and went into his hut and shut the door. A bubble of smoke, pink and shining, floated out of the chimney

and hung in the air, lighting up the jungle all around. Holding the paper bag carefully in his scaly paw, Lassie heaved himself out of the water and waddled over to the trees.

It is not easy collecting the seeds of rare and valuable orchids when you have two large paws each with three golden knife-like claws, and only a very small paper bag to put the seeds in. The young dragon knew that

seeds should always be left on the plant to make new plants. But this was a magic island and the seeds and roots grew again the moment Lassie gathered them.

The bag looked no bigger from the outside, but somehow there was always room for another seed or root. It was a fiddly and difficult task for a young dragon. In the end he found the easiest method was to nip off the seed-heads with his mouth and spit the seeds carefully into the paper bag.

He sat back on his plump tail and sucked and spat – just like you might eat cherries and spit the stones – for a long, long time, until the stars faded and the great orange tropical moon went down behind the darkness of the jungle trees. Even then, Lassie carried on collecting his seeds, and carefully, very carefully, digging and cutting roots lit by the shining pink bubble of smoke which hung above Meehort's hut.

When the morning sun came up in a rush of yellow heat Lassie had finished. In his hand he had a bag filled with orchid seeds and orchid roots. It was a wonderful collection – more rare flowers than anyone had ever collected before. He paddled back down the

river, nibbling at flowers as he went, and then he sat for a little while on the golden beach, watching the turquoise waves rolling in and washing against the shore.

When he was rested, the young dragon took his paper bag firmly in one paw, and flung himself in a great gallop along the sandy beach, beating his wings and straining to leap upwards. With a few great strides he made it!

The warm currents of air from the island lifted him upwards and he circled around looking down. Below him was the stream and Meehort's hut, and Meehort's pink smoke bubble. Lassie waved a paw to the hut and the smoke bubble waved back and popped. Lassie turned his head for the north, stretched out his body in the warm air, and beat his wings steadily and strongly, heading for James and home.

Chapter 6

James was rounding the corner into his street, trailing his school bag behind him, when the sun was suddenly blocked, and a great shadow fell on him and then passed down the street.

James looked up into the sky and let out a shriek which had his mam and dad tumbling out of their front door to see what was the matter. There, in the sky above the street, at roof-top height, Lassie was circling, trying to land. He had the knack of it now. He lined himself up with the road like a jumbo jet lines up with a runway. He flew slower and slower, sank down to about two metres off the ground and then dropped like a small avalanche. The street rocked slightly, but nothing was actually broken.

James pelted forward and flung his arms around Lassie's great neck.

"Lassie!" James's mam called, and she ran outside with a handful of rose petals to welcome him home.

Lassie carefully laid the paper bag at their feet and beamed at them.

"What's this?" James asked. He opened the bag and looked inside. "It's only seeds," he said, disappointed. "And roots and things. Why did you bring us these, Lassie?"

James's dad took the bag and looked in. James could see his face changing. First he looked surprised, then he looked amazed, and then his face crumpled as if he might laugh aloud or cry. "Seeds," he said, "and fresh roots! Orchid seeds and roots!"

He looked at Lassie. "Where have you been?" he asked. "Where did you get them? This is the most amazing collection I have ever seen in my life!"

Lassie's eyes beamed a bright ruby colour. He did not say anything. He could not say anything.

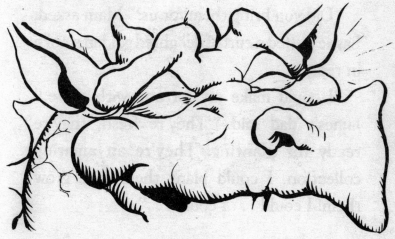

"Did you bring them for us?" Mam asked. Lassie puffed a curl of delighted golden smoke in reply.

"I could make my fortune with these," James's dad said. "They're fresh, they're ready for planting. They're an amazing collection. I could plant them, and grow them! I could . . . I could . . ."

James put his arm over his dragon's neck and watched his dad. His dad looked somehow different. He looked taller, he looked younger. He was pink with excitement and stammering.

"We could plant them in pots and keep them in the house," he said. "If we turned the whole of the upstairs into a greenhouse . . . I suppose we could grow them . . ."

James's mam was smiling at James's dad with love in her eyes. "We can't plant them in the house, pet," she said gently. "There isn't room."

"Then I'll build a greenhouse!" James's dad said determinedly. "This is the chance of a lifetime for us and we are going to take it.

Lassie has brought us a miracle. An absolute miracle! Somewhere, somehow I'm going to get a greenhouse and make these flowers grow!"

Lassie leaned forward and gave James a poke in the shoulder with his bony nose. James turned around. Lassie was beaming at him, his eyes bright. A little curl of smoke came from each nostril.

"What?" James asked.

Lassie's rosy eyes implored James to think. He puffed a tiny cloud of smoke into James's face and James stepped back from the heat.

"What?" James said again. Then he yelled, "Of course! I see! It's brilliant! You're a genius! A genius, Lassie!"

He grabbed hold of his mam's hand and his
dad's arm. His dad kept tight hold of the bag
of plants and Lassie galloped before them as
James towed his mam and dad down the
garden path, through the back garden,
through the little gate into their allotment,
and across all the allotments to the old
greenhouse which stood empty and cold in
the corner of the site.

The door hung open and a few panes of glass were broken. The boiler was rusty and damp in the corner. James darted towards it and flung open the boiler door. It was filled with old wet coke stuck together in a hopeless cold lump. It had been years and years since the boiler had been lit – years and years since the greenhouse had been warm.

"Go on!" James yelled, jumping up and down in delight. "Go on!"

James's mam and dad looked at each other in amazement, but Lassie and James understood each other. Lassie bent his great snouty head towards the open door of the boiler, and with a beaming smile as broad as a crocodile's grin he blew a deep, burning blast of breath into the very heart of the boiler.

At once it caught light and began to warm up. The coke glowed bright as a furnace. Little whispers of steam came from vents in the walls. The greenhouse windows, all thickly misted with the damp of many years, started to steam and clear. The pipes all around the greenhouse clicked as they warmed. Somewhere a tap dripped – a lush, wet springlike sound.

"Yes!" James's dad cried out. "Yes! This would do for my plants all right!"

"And Will Groves's tomatoes," James's mam said.

"And everybody's early seedlings," James's dad added excitedly. "It's such a huge greenhouse and it belongs to the allotments – everyone should use it. We could all repair it, we could help each other. If Lassie would heat it for us . . ." he hesitated. "*Would* you heat it for us, Lassie?"

Lassie's eyes glowed as bright as the coals. He nodded delightedly. Then he rolled his head towards James like a cat wanting a stroke.

James flung his arms around his pet's hot, scaly neck.

"Was there ever a dog like this?" he demanded.

James's mam and dad called a meeting of everyone in the street, and all of them (even miserable Mr Perkins next door) agreed that they would get together and rebuild the greenhouse, and together grow flowers, vegetables and plants.

James's mam gave up her cleaning job and worked in the greenhouse with James's dad and the other neighbours. She stopped smelling of cleaning polish and her face grew brown and sunny instead of white and tired. In the first year they made enough money to pay everyone a proper wage, and in the second year they made a small profit. In a little while the allotments and greenhouse became quite famous and they called themselves Dragon Plants in honour of Lassie.

They always have the earliest flowering plants of any garden centre, because they keep their greenhouse so hot. Even in midwinter you can buy roses and strawberries from the Dragon Plants shop. Even at

Christmas you can buy fresh rare flowers. The beautiful rich ladies of Yorkshire and Durham send to Dragon Plants for orchids to pin to their evening dresses, and flowers to perfume their rooms. Sometimes they come to the shop and walk around the greenhouses. They give James's dad enormous orders for plants and pay with huge cheques.

Sometimes they pat James on the head and call him "perfectly sweet", and he has learned to smile and not make sick noises.

Sometimes things go wrong in the greenhouse. They have had their failures. Once they lost a whole tray of seedlings because they got too hot and dry, and one lady complained that her roses were scorched, as if they had been near smoke – but that was obviously impossible. They told her that they could not imagine how the petals had got so hot and crumpled, and they gave her a fresh bouquet.

James has a little sister now, and when his mam is working in the greenhouse she often puts the pram out in the garden. She is a happy baby and never cries, for there is

always someone to rock her to sleep. Someone once said they thought they saw a large
green tail tipping the pram gently to and fro.
But that is obviously impossible too. It must
have been an odd trick of the light.

James still does not have a bike, although
he is now eleven. But he does not mind at all.
Who wants to cycle when you and all your
friends can climb on to the great green back
of your very own dragon, and fly higher and
higher in the sky, all the way to the South
Seas, where the water turns as blue as

bluebells, as blue as delphiniums, and then as blue as violets, and there is a secret island, unknown to any map, and a wizard called Meehort who always has your favourite tea ready and waiting for you?